Mother Goose Asks "Why?"

Introducing Families to Science
through Great Children's Literature

HOME LOVELY

BY LYNNE RAE PERKINS

GREENWILLOW BOOKS  NEW YORK

Pen and ink and watercolor paints were used for the full-color art. The text type is Novarese BT.

Printed in Singapore by KHL Printing Co. Pte. Ltd.
First Edition   10 9 8 7 6 5 4

Library of Congress Cataloging-in-Publication Data

Perkins, Lynne Rae.
Home lovely / by Lynne Rae Perkins.
    p.   cm.
Summary: Hoping for trees or a flower garden, Tiffany transplants and cares for some seedlings that she finds and is surprised by what they become.
ISBN 0-688-13687-7 (trade).   ISBN 0-688-13688-5 (lib. bdg.)
[1. Gardening—Fiction.]   I. Title.   PZ7.P4313Ho   1995
[E]—dc20   94-21917   CIP   AC

For my father,

who was

a kind person

like Bob

Tiffany and her mom, Janelle, had to move at the end of May.
Not only did they have to move at the end of May,

but they had to move into a trailer that wasn't in a trailer
park, or in a town, or even near any kind of a house
as far as Tiffany could see. And Janelle had to go to work.

Janelle had to go to work for a few hours in the afternoons. That's just how it was, and she couldn't afford a babysitter. So Tiffany was supposed to keep the doors locked and stay inside, although she could open as many windows as she wanted.

"Watch TV," said Janelle. "Play with your dolls. Have a snack. I'll be back before you know it."

At first that's just what Tiffany did. She watched TV, she changed Barbie's clothes about a million times, she ate orange Popsicles. Once she phoned Janelle at work and they had a nice long chat, but Janelle's boss said she couldn't do that too often.

Then one day after supper Tiffany was taking out the
garbage when she spied some little seedlings growing.
"I think there are some little trees growing in our
backyard," she told her mother. "Or they might be
flowers. I'm not sure."
"No kidding?" said Janelle. "Where?"
"Out by the garbage can," Tiffany answered. "Is it okay if
I move them to the front yard? Maybe by the driveway?"

"Sure," said Janelle. "Maybe around the porch, too. This place looks so bare. You know, you have to water plants to keep them alive."

"I know," said Tiffany. "Do you think I need to make a scarecrow?"

"Probably not right away. Besides, I think that's for corn."

Early the next morning, while Janelle was still snoozing, Tiffany got to work. There seemed to be three kinds of flowers or trees, so she planted one of each and then started over—to make a pattern. They looked spread apart, but you don't want to put trees too close together. She watered them carefully, then went inside to have some cream-cheese tortillas.

She spent that afternoon reading about some princess's garden in one of Janelle's *Home Lovely* magazines.

"A garden pleases the eye and is a companion to the soul," the magazine said.

That's true, thought Tiffany.

type #1:

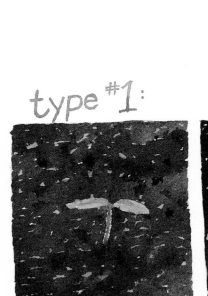
at first

later

now

type #2:

at first

later

now

type #3:

at first   later   now

Days and weeks
went by, and the
little plants grew .
and grew. You could
really tell the three
types apart now.
Each was so beautiful
in its own way.

One especially hot morning Tiffany was out watering plants when the mail carrier stopped at the mailbox, then got out to take a closer look.

"You have some good-looking tomatoes there," he said cheerfully.

"Huh?" said Tiffany.

"Melons don't look too bad either. The potatoes are real pretty, but you never can tell about them till you dig them up," he said.

"Potatoes?" asked Tiffany.

"Yeah, these right here, these potatoes. Right alongside the driveway is an unusual place to put a vegetable garden. Not a bad idea, though—you can keep your eye on it that way."

"These are vegetables?" asked Tiffany. "I was hoping they were flowers. Or maybe trees."

"Nope," said the mail carrier. "Even better. You can't eat flowers and trees."

"Huh," said Tiffany.

She was still mourning the loss of her flowers and trees
when Janelle came home from work.

"But, honey," said Janelle, "this is great. Tomatoes and
cantaloupe are my favorites. And you lo-o-o-ove
french fries."

"Oh, sweetie," Janelle said, "they're pretty. And I think
they still get flowers sometimes."

"Hey, I know," Janelle said. "Let's make a scarecrow."
So they ransacked their drawers and closets, and put
together a fabulous scarecrow.

A day or so later the mail carrier, whose name was Bob, stopped to admire the new addition. And speaking of additions, he had a little tray of them for Tiffany's garden.

"These are marigolds," he said, "and these are pansies, and these are petunias. Maybe you can find some room for them on the edge of your vegetables."

"Wow," said Tiffany. "You brought these for me?"

"Oh, I just had a few extras," said Bob. "Thought maybe you could use them."

"I sure can," said Tiffany. She inspected the purple, pink, and orange blooms. "These are the most beautiful flowers I've ever seen. These are as beautiful as Princess Alexandra's garden. Thanks, Bob."

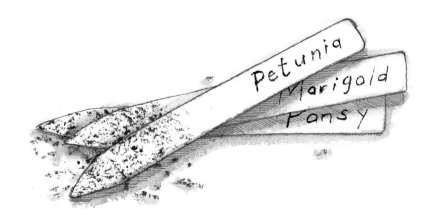

After that, Bob stopped frequently to check on the garden and to give tips on how to make it grow better. For example, he told Tiffany about tying the tomatoes to stakes as they got taller and heavier.

Tiffany figured she didn't need her socks until fall, and then the tomatoes wouldn't need them anymore.

Bob would stop at their mailbox around noon,
just before Janelle left for work. So sometimes
Janelle would fix everyone a Coke, and they
would all take a little rest on the porch.

It was a big day when Tiffany picked the first red tomato from the vine.

"B.L.T.s all around!" yelled Janelle. It was August now, and
hot as heck, but that seemed fine as the unbelievably
sweet and tasty tomatoes melted in their mouths.
"My, my," said Bob.

The week before school started, Janelle took Tiffany to the mall for some new clothes—especially socks. They had lunch and talked about school and Janelle's job, which was going to be full time now. That would help out a lot with bills, and they celebrated by having sundaes, buying nail polish, and going to the movies.

When they returned home, there was
something standing in the driveway.
It was a little tree, with a ball-shaped
bottom wrapped in burlap.
A note was tied to a branch:

Fall is a good time
for planting trees.
Bob

"That Bob!" said Janelle.
And she and Tiffany laughed
and went inside to make
Tomatoes Romanoff for supper
and Floating Melon Bonanza
for dessert.